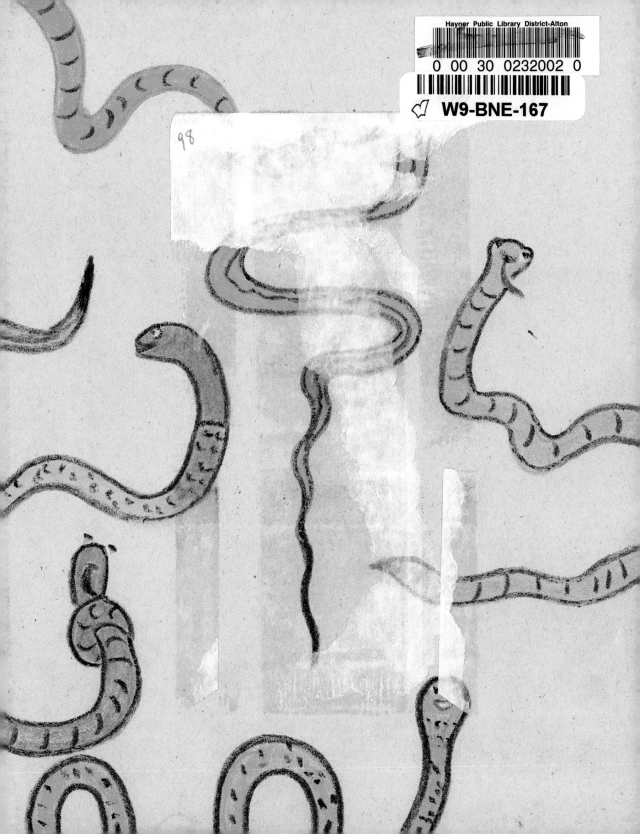

To Rob, who needed a snake
and found his own
—LJ

For Crictor and Madame Bodot
—PM

Text copyright © 1998 by Lynne Jonell. Illustrations copyright © 1998 by Petra Mathers
All rights reserved. This book, or parts thereof, may not be reproduced in any form
without permission in writing from the publisher. G. P. Putnam's Sons, a division of
The Putnam & Grosset Group, 200 Madison Avenue, New York, NY 10016.
G. P. Putnam's Sons, Reg. U.S. Pat. & Tm. Off.
Published simultaneously in Canada. Printed and bound in Singapore.
Book designed by Cecilia Yung and Donna Mark. Text set in Catchup.
Library of Congress Cataloging-in-Publication Data
Jonell, Lynne. I need a snake/written by Lynne Jonell; illustrated by Petra Mathers.
p. cm. Summary: A young boy really wants a snake of his own, and after
his mother reads a book about snakes and takes him to a museum and
a pet store to see some, he finds his own pet "snakes" around the house.
[1. Snakes—Fiction. 2. Mothers and sons—Fiction.] I. Mathers, Petra, ill.
II. Title. PZ7.J675Iaam 1998 [E]—dc21 97-30148 CIP AC
ISBN 0-399-23176-5
1 3 5 7 9 10 8 6 4 2
First Impression

WRITTEN BY Lynne Jonell
ILLUSTRATED BY Petra Mathers

G. P. PUTNAM'S SONS   NEW YORK

Robbie had toys.
Robbie had books.
But Robbie did not have a snake.

"I need a snake," he said.
"I need a snake **now**."

Mommy shook her head.
"Snakes are dangerous. And scary."
"That is why I need one," said Robbie.
"Hmmm," said Mommy. "Maybe we could
read a **book** about snakes."

Robbie looked at the snake book.
The pictures were wonderful.
"Why does the snake eat the mouse
headfirst?" he asked.

Mommy looked slightly sick.
"Can I have a snake **now**?" Robbie asked.
"Not today," said Mommy.

"Tomorrow?" asked Robbie.
"Let's go to the museum tomorrow,"
said Mommy. "We can see
a real snake there."

The museum was a big and dusty place.
"Here are the snakes," said Mommy.
"See how many?"
"But why don't they move?" asked Robbie.
"Because they are stuffed," said Mommy.

"Stuffed snakes are not alive."
"What good is a snake that
doesn't wiggle?" asked Robbie.
Mommy sighed. "I guess we could go to
a pet store," she said. "Just to look."

Robbie loved the pet store.
The snakes were big. They were slithery.
They had small black tongues that
flicked in and out.

"May I help you?" said a man with a tattoo.
"We are just looking," said Mommy.
"But I want this one!" cried Robbie.

"Not now," said Mommy.
"When?" said Robbie.

"When you are all grown up," said Mommy.
"When you have a house of your own."

"That is too long to wait," said Robbie.
"Not long enough," said Mommy.
"I need one right now," said Robbie.
Mommy did not answer.

"I guess I will have to find one
by myself," said Robbie.
It did not take him very long.
He found a little white snake in
his mother's closet.

It was a nice snake, but too wiggly.
"You'll have to calm down if you want me
to carry you," said Robbie,
and he stroked it with a gentle finger.

He found the next snake hiding
under his sister's bed.

It was a lovely, sparkly green, but it tried
to bite him when he pulled it out.
Robbie shook it by the tail.
"If you act poisonous, no one will
like you," he warned.

The last snake was the best.
Robbie found it wrapped around his
father's pants. It was big.
It was black with a gold head.
And it was very dangerous.

"I will not hurt you," said Robbie.
"But no squeezing without permission."

The black snake hissed and hissed.
But Robbie made it obey.

And when Mommy came in, looking for
her shoelace, and Sister's green jump
rope, and Father's new belt, the big black
snake only bent its gold head and
clicked its fangs. And the green snake
just wriggled and danced, showing off
its beautiful sparkles.

And the little white snake slithered
down from Robbie's shoulder onto
Mommy's hand, where it
coiled itself up with a small,
friendly hiss.

"You see?" said Robbie. "Snakes can be
very nice pets, if you know how to
make them behave."

"I guess you are right," said Mommy.
"But I still think they are scary."
"That is why you need me," said Robbie.

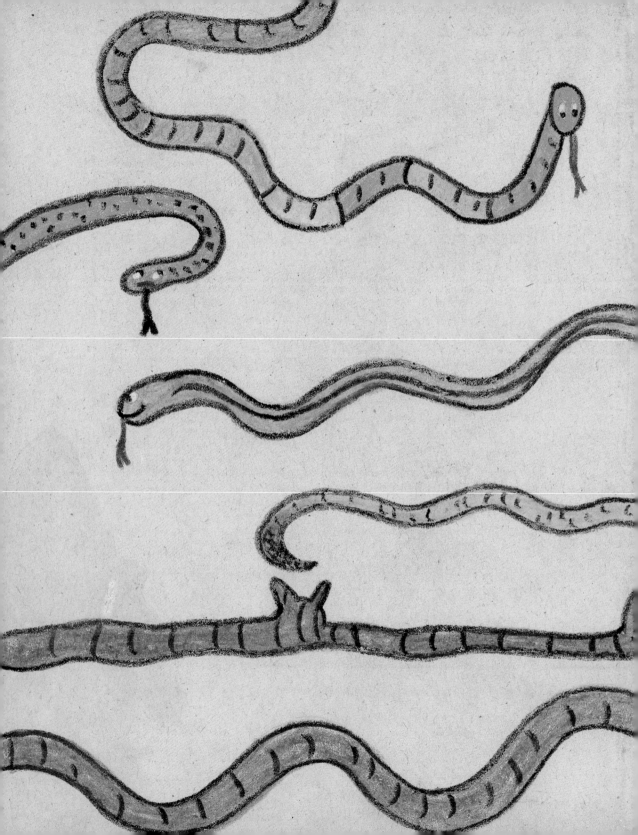